To MY DaD ♥ and HIS
≡ FANTASTIC ≡ Bull
who SAT like
a DOG

Bloomsbury Publishing, London, New Delhi, New York and Sydney
First published in Great Britain in 2015 by Bloomsbury Publishing Plc
50 Bedford Square, London, WC1B 3DP

Text/illustrations copyright © Catalina Echeverri 2015
The moral right of the author/illustrator has been asserted

A CIP catalogue record for this book is available from the British Library

ISBN 978 1 4088 3879 2 (HB)
ISBN 978 1 4088 3880 8 (PB)
ISBN 978 1 4088 3878 5 (eBook)
Printed in China by Leo Paper Products, Heshan, Guangdong

1 3 5 7 9 10 8 6 4 2

www.bloomsbury.com

All papers used by Bloomsbury Publishing are natural, recyclable products
made from wood grown in well-managed forests.
The manufacturing processes conform to the environmental regulations of the country of origin

BLOOMSBURY is a registered trademark of Bloomsbury Publishing Plc

MILO'S DOG SAYS MOO!

Catalina Echeverri

Hello everyone! I'm Milo.
It's my birthday today – not an ordinary
birthday, a super extra-special birthday.
Do you want to know why?
Because I'm getting my very own dog.
I even get to pick it myself!
Would you like to come along?

BLOOMSBURY
LONDON   NEW DELHI   NEW YORK   SYDNEY

As you can see, I've been **very** busy getting **everything** ready for the arrival of my new **dog**.

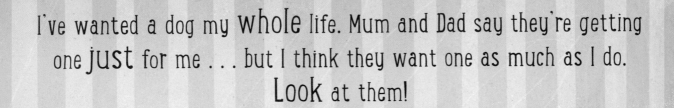

I've wanted a dog my **whole** life. Mum and Dad say they're getting one **just** for me . . . but I think they want one as much as I do. **Look** at them!

Mum thinks my new dog should be small and have a **fancy** haircut. Dad thinks it should be able to give good doggy **kisses**.

But . . .

"I want this one!" I say.

"His name is Beans."

"But he's so much **bigger** than all the others," says Mum.
"He's definitely . . . **unique**," says Dad.
"Are you **sure**, Milo?"

"Dad, Beans is **perfect**!
The most wonderful dog in the WHOOOOLE world!" I say.

"OK . . . if you're **really** sure?" says Dad.

Yippee!

Back home, Beans gets a **special** tour of the house. He seems to like Mum's **plants** the best.

At dinnertime, I give Beans a
HUGE bowl of Super Dog food,
but he doesn't seem very hungry.
Maybe he is just too excited to eat.

The next day, we start Beans' dog lessons.

I take him for a **walk**.

I show him how to S-I-T.

We even have time to play fetch.
Well, sort of.

Beans, look! The ball!

But Beans isn't like **other** dogs.

He doesn't **chew** on **bones**.

He thinks it's more **fun** to **play** with cats than to **chase** them.

And he is terrible at barking.

But there is **one** thing,
Beans is **very** good at . . .

getting bigger . . .

and bigger . . .

BEANS

BEANS

and bigger.

In fact, Beans is growing SO quickly, he doesn't
fit through our front door anymore!
So with the help of Mum and Dad, I build a cosy new home
for him in the garden. Beans loves being outside!

It makes me happy to see Beans SO happy.

But the next morning, I get a **shock**. Beans is **gone**. He's **eaten** his way through our garden, and our neighbour's garden, and our neighbour's neighbour's garden! And when we follow the muddy tracks we find . . .

We look and look until Mum and
Dad say we have to go home.
"Maybe Beans is where he belongs now," says Dad.
"But Beans belongs with us," I say.

So I call him one last time . . .

Beans!

Then, all of a sudden,
I hear a familiar . . .

mooooooo!

Could it be?

It is!

This is my dog, Beans.
He's not **at all** like **other** dogs but
I **love** Beans and Beans **loves** me.
And we'll be **friends forever**.